W9-DCD-626

Friendship Goals

by C.L. Reid

illustrated by Elena Aiello

PICTURE WINDOW BOOKS
a capstone imprint

Published by Picture Window Books, an imprint of Capstone
1710 Roe Crest Drive, North Mankato, Minnesota 56003
capstonepub.com

Library of Congress Cataloging-in-Publication Data
Names: Reid, C. L., author. | Aiello, Elena (Illustrator), illustrator. Title:
Friendship goals / by C. L. Reid ; illustrated by Elena Aiello.
Description: North Mankato, Minnesota : Picture Window Books,
an imprint of Capstone, 2021. | Series: Emma every day |
Audience: Ages 5–7. | Audience: Grades K–1. |
Summary: Emma, who is deaf and wears a cochlear implant,
loves playing soccer with her friends Izzie and Chen, but when
Izzie gets discouraged and wants to quit, Emma and Chen
take the time to show her that improvement comes through
practice. Includes discussion questions, writing prompts, an
ASL fingerspelling chart, and a sign language guide.
Identifiers: LCCN 2021006189 (print) | LCCN 2021006190 (ebook) |
ISBN 9781663909268 (hardcover) | ISBN 9781663921932 (paperback) |
ISBN 9781663909237 (pdf) Subjects: CYAC: Soccer—Fiction. | Friendship—
Fiction. | Perseverance (Ethics)—Fiction. | Deaf—Fiction. | Cochlear
implants—Fiction. | People with disabilities—Fiction. Classification: LCC
PZ7.1.R4544 Fr 2021 (print) | LCC PZ7.1.R4544 (ebook) | DDC [E]—dc23
LC record available at https://lccn.loc.gov/2021006189
LC ebook record available at https://lccn.loc.gov/2021006190

Image Credits: Capstone: Daniel Griffo, 29, Margeaux Lucas, 28 top right,
Mick Reid, 28 bottom, Randy Chewning, 28 top left

Design Elements: Shutterstock: achii, Mari C, Mika Besfamilnaya

Special thanks to Evelyn Keolian for her consulting work.

Designer: Tracy Davies

TABLE OF CONTENTS

MEET EMMA

EMMA CARTER
Age: 8 Grade: 3

SIBLING
one brother, Jaden
(12 years old)

PARENTS
David and Lucy

BEST FRIEND
Izzie Jackson

PET
a goldfish named Ruby

favorite color: teal
favorite food: tacos
favorite school subject: writing
favorite sport: swimming
hobbies: reading, writing, biking, swimming

FINGERSPELLING GUIDE

MANUAL ALPHABET

Aa Bb Cc Dd Ee

Ff Gg Hh Ii Jj

MANUAL NUMBERS

0 1 2 3

Emma is Deaf. She uses American Sign Language (ASL) to communicate with her family. She also uses a cochlear implant (CI) to help her hear some sounds.

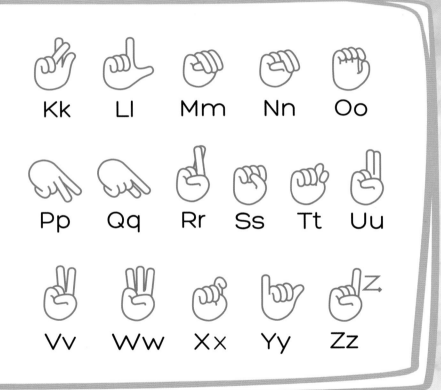

Kk   Ll   Mm   Nn   Oo

Pp   Qq   Rr   Ss   Tt   Uu

Vv   Ww   Xx   Yy   Zz

4   5   6   7   8   9   10

Chapter 1
Pep Talk

The team finished its last lap.

Then everyone plopped down on

the bench. Soccer practice was over.

Coach was ready to talk. Emma pressed a button on her cochlear implant (CI) to change the program so she could hear better.

"Good practice, team," Coach said. "We're definitely ready for our first game on Saturday. Huddle up!"

"Let's go!"  everyone

yelled.

Everyone except for Izzie.

She didn't join the cheering.

Chen joined Emma and Izzie as they walked to their car.

"You don't look happy," he said to Izzie.

"I'm terrible at soccer. I want to quit," Izzie said.

"You can't quit. Let's practice at the park  after school. We have three days until the game," Emma signed.

"I'll give it a try," Izzie said.

"I will help too," Chen said.

"I can practice my soccer and my signing."

"Sounds good," Emma signed.

Chapter 2

Practice, Practice, Practice

The next day after school, the three friends met at the park.

"Let's pass the ball to each other," Emma signed.

She put the ball on the ground
and passed it to Chen. Chen passed
it to Izzie. Izzie missed the ball.

"I am not good," she signed.

"Focus on the ball," Emma
signed. "You can do it."

She passed the ball to Izzie. Izzie missed again.

"I'll never get it!" Izzie said.

"Keep trying," Chen said.

Chen passed the ball to Izzie.

Wham! 🤚✌️🤏👋 Izzie kicked

the ball hard. It flew into the air

and bounced way off the field.

"You didn't miss it that time!"

Emma signed, laughing.

"You just need more practice,"

Chen signed.

"I agree, and I will not give up,"

Izzie signed.

"Let's meet here tomorrow at the

same time," Emma signed.

The next day Emma said, "Let's practice kicking the ball into the goal first."

Chen passed the ball to Izzie. Izzie ran after it but tripped on the ball.

"Ugh!"  Izzie signed.

"You can do it," Chen said.

They tried again. Chen passed

the ball to Izzie. This time Izzie

kicked it way off the field.

"I want to quit," Izzie signed.

"No way," Emma signed. "You are getting better. Use the side of your foot and keep trying."

Chapter 3
Goals

On Friday Izzie signed, "I am still not sure about soccer."

"Let's try kicking it into the goal again," Emma signed.

Emma passed the ball to Chen. Chen passed it to Izzie.

Izzie ran after it as fast as she could. Then she kicked it right into the goal!

"Whoopee!"  Chen yelled.

"I did it!" Izzie said.

After that they practiced some more. Izzie got better with every kick.

Saturday morning was bright and cool. It was a perfect day for a soccer game. Emma put on her CI and her uniform.

"Wish us luck," she said to Ruby, her pet goldfish.

Then she grabbed her soccer bag
and headed downstairs.

"You ready for the game?" her
mom signed.

"Yes!" Emma signed. "I think
Izzie is ready too."

At the soccer field, Emma found
Izzie and Chen. They looked excited.

"I am a little nervous, but I am
ready," Izzie signed.

"Practice pays off," Chen signed.

"Thanks for all your help,"

Izzie signed.

"That is what friends are for,"

Emma signed.

LEARN TO SIGN

ball

Bring fingers together.

game

Make A shape and tap
knuckles together twice.

soccer

Hit bottom
hand twice.

run

Hook thumb and index finger
and move hands forward.

friend

1. Lock fingers.
2. Repeat with other hand on top.

applause

Twist hands near face.

fast

Bend fingers as you
move hands up.

GLOSSARY

cochlear implant (also called CI)—a device that helps someone who is Deaf to hear; it is worn on the head just above the ear

deaf—being unable to hear

fingerspell—to make letters with your hands to spell out words; often used for names of people and places

huddle—to gather in a small group or circle

nervous—feeling worried

pass—to kick a ball to a teammate

sign language—a language in which hand gestures, along with facial expressions and body movements, are used to communicate

TALK ABOUT IT

1. Izzie wanted to quit soccer because it was hard for her. Have you ever felt that way about something? What did you do?

2. How do you think Izzie felt when she was practicing at the park with her friends?

3. Do you think Izzie kept playing soccer after the game, or did she end up quitting? Talk about your answer.

WRITE ABOUT IT

1. Emma loves to play soccer. Write about an activity that you love to do.

2. Emma and Chen are good friends to Izzie. Make a list of five ways you can be a good friend.

3. Pretend you are a reporter. Write an article about who won the soccer game.

Ruby

ABOUT THE AUTHOR

Deaf-blind since childhood, C.L. Reid received a cochlear implant (CI) as an adult to help her hear, and she uses American Sign Language (ASL) to communicate. She and her husband have three sons. Their middle son is also deaf-blind. C.L. earned a master's degree in writing for children and young adults at Hamline University in St. Paul, Minnesota. She lives in Minnesota with her husband, two of their sons, and their cats.

ABOUT THE ILLUSTRATOR

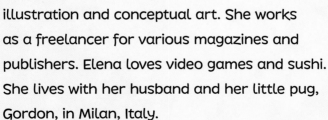

Elena Aiello is an illustrator and character designer. After graduating as a marketing specialist, she decided to study art direction and CGI. Doing so, she discovered a passion for illustration and conceptual art. She works as a freelancer for various magazines and publishers. Elena loves video games and sushi. She lives with her husband and her little pug, Gordon, in Milan, Italy.